A GRASSHOPPER NAMED SCOOT

A Frontier Creative Studios book.

Published by Frontier Creative Studios
Text copyright © 2020 by Charlotte Pearce
Illustration copyright © 2020 Misha Skinner-Gehr

1st printing.

Pearce, Charlotte, 1943-
A Grasshopper Named Scoot

ISBN-13: 978-1-7354775-0-3

Published in the United States by Frontier Creative Studios.

Design: Misha Skinner-Gehr

Printed in the United States.

For Oona Imogen

This is a story about Scoot
the Grasshopper.

All of Scoot's brothers and sisters
were excellent jumpers.

Scoot was the only one
who did not jump.

Both his Father and Mother would gently encourage him.

His brothers and sisters made fun of him.

Scoot was not going to jump no matter what!

He would only scoot along the ground.

Scoot's Mother took him to the Grasshopper Doctor to see if maybe he had some nerve damage that happened during birth.

Nope, Scoot was just fine.

Then she took him to a Jumpologist to see if his muscles were strained.

All the muscles were just fine.

She even tried a Stubbornologist to see if this was a problem with attitude, but that didn't help either.

Scoot's Mother scratched her head so hard trying to figure out what was wrong that she almost caused her antennae to fall out.

Mother tried speaking calmly to Scoot.

"Scoot, my beloved insect child, you must learn to jump because that is how you catch food and how you avoid being stepped on."

Mother tried time-outs, crying, yelling, begging, pleading, bribes and every single Mom-trick she knew until she was at her wit's end.

Nothing worked.

Scoot refused to change. He would not jump.

Mother loved Scoot so much and was not going to give up. That's just the way Moms are.

One day Mother had an idea how she might help her
son.

She had Scoot sit next to her. She
didn't say anything.

She took a small pebble
and she threw it into the air.

The pebble
went wwwwaaaaaaaaaayyy up and then it plopped
down. She did this
several times.

Mother looked at Scoot and said,

"Isn't that interesting? No matter how hard I throw the pebble, it always comes down."

Scoot looked at Mother with big fat tears in his little grasshopper eyes.

"Mother, I don't want to hop so high that I won't ever see you again."

He was afraid if he jumped too high, he would keep on going

until he went
past the moon

and all of
the planets

He was afraid he would go beyond the edge of the solar system

and out of the universe and
would never find his way home.

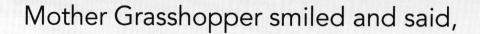

Mother Grasshopper smiled and said,

"Oh, Scoot, that is so sweet. Gravity and your love will always keep you close by until you are really ready to jump away from home."

With that, they hugged each other.

Scoot became one of best darn jumpers in the
world.

And he never jumped so high that he couldn't come back.

The End.

Charlotte Pearce is an artist and writer living in Eugene, Oregon. She spends a good portion of her time playing with alcohol inks, encaustic wax and mosaicking. When she doesn't have her hands covered in ink or grout or wax, she spends time writing stories for children. She also enjoys watching hummingbirds on her balcony, a hot cup of tea and hanging out with her granddaughter.

Misha S. Gehr is an illustrator and writer who lives in Portland, Oregon, where she works on comics, illustration, and novels. She has had a passion for storytelling for most of her life, studying film and writing in high school, and majoring in creative writing and comics at Portland State University. She is the founder of Frontier Creative Studios, and in her free time she enjoys reading, tea, and gardening.